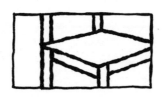

NADINE GORDIMER

Harald, Claudia, and their son Duncan

A
BLOOMSBURY
QUID

First published in Great Britain 1996

Copyright © 1996 by Nadine Gordimer

The moral right of the author has been asserted

Bloomsbury Publishing Plc,
2 Soho Square, London W1V 6HB

A CIP catalogue record for this book
is available from the British Library

ISBN 0 7475 2891 8

Typeset by Hewer Text Composition Services, Edinburgh
Printed by St Edmundsbury Press, Suffolk
Jacket design by Jeff Fisher

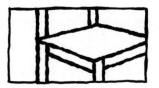

Something terrible happened.

They are watching it on the screen with their after-dinner coffee cups beside them. It is Bosnia or Somalia or the earthquake shaking a Japanese island like a dog between apocalyptic teeth; whatever were the disasters of that time. The screen serves them up with coffee every night. When the intercom buzzes each looks to the other with a friendly reluctance: you go, your turn. It's part of the covenant of

3

living together. They made the decision to give up the house and move into this town-house complex with grounds maintained and security-monitored entrance only recently and they are not yet accustomed, or rather are inclined momentarily to forget that it's not the barking of Robbie and the old-fangled ring of the front door bell that summons them, now. No pets allowed in the complex, but luckily there was the solution that theirs could go to their son who has a garden cottage.

He/she – twitch of a smile, he got himself up with languor directed at her and went to lift the nearest receiver. Who, she half-heard him say, half-listening to the commentary following the images, Who. It could be someone wanting to convert them to some religious sect, or the delivery of a summons for a parking offence; moonlighting workers did this. He said something else she didn't catch but she heard the release buzzer he pressed.

Do you know who Julian Verster might be? Friend of Duncan?

He/she – they didn't, either of them. Nothing unusual about that. Duncan, thirty years old, had his own circle just as his parents had theirs, and these intersected only occasionally where interests, inculcated in him as a child by his parents, met.

What does he want?

Just said to speak to us.

Both at the same instant were touched by a live voltage of alarm. What is there to fear, defined in the known context of a thirty year old in this city – a car crash, a street mugging, a violent break-in at the cottage. Both stood at the door, confronting these, confronting the footsteps they followed approaching up their private paved pathway beneath the crossed swords of Strelitzia palm leaves, the signal of the second buzzer, and this young man come from? For? Duncan. It doesn't matter what he looked like. He stared at the floor as he came in, so they couldn't read him. He sat down without a word; it was an injunction for them to do so, too.

He/she – whose turn. There's been an accident? – she's a doctor, she sees what the ambulances bring into Intensive Care. If something's broken she can gauge whether it ever can be put together again.

This Julian draws the flaps of his lips in over his teeth and clamps his mouth before he speaks.

A kind of . . . Not Duncan, no no! Someone's been shot. Duncan, he's been arrested.

They stand up. For God's sake – what are you talking about – What is all this – How arrested, arrested for what –

The messenger is attacked, he

becomes sullen, unable to bear what he has to tell. The obscene word comes ashamedly from him.

Murder.

Everything has come to a stop.

What can be understood is only a car crash, a street mugging, a violent break-in.

He/she. He strides over and switches off the television. And expels a violent breath. So long as nobody moved, nobody uttered, the word and the act within the word could not enter here. Now with the touch of a switch and the gush of breath a new calendar is opened. The old Gregorian cannot register this day. It does not exist in that means of measure.

This Julian now tells them that a magistrate was called 'after hours' (he gives the detail with the weight of its urgent gravity) to lay a charge at the police station and bail was refused. That is the practical purpose of this visit: Duncan says – Duncan says, Duncan's message is that there's no point in their coming, there's no point in trying for bail, he will appear in court on Monday morning. He has his own lawyer.

He/she. She has marked the date on patients' prescriptions dozens of times since morning but she turns to find a question that will bring some kind of answer to that word pronounced by the messenger. She cries out. *What day is it today?*

Friday.

It was on a Friday.

It is probable that neither of the Linmeyers had ever been in a court before. During the forty-eight hours of the weekend of waiting they had gone over every explanation possible in the absence of being able to talk to him, their son, himself. Because of the preposterousness of the charge they felt they had to respect his instruction that they not try to see him; this must indicate that the whole business was ridiculous, that's it, horribly ridiculous, his own ridiculous affair soon to be resolved, better not given the confirmation of being taken seriously by mother and

father arriving at a prison accompa-
nied by their lawyer, high emotions,
etc. That was the way they brought
themselves to read his injunction; a
mixture between consideration of
them – no need to be mixed up in
the business – and the independence
of the young he had been granted in
mutual understanding and asserted
since he was an adolescent.

But dread attends the unknown.
Dread was a drug that came to them
both not out of something adminis-
tered from her pharmacopoeia; they
calmly walked without anything to
say to one another along the corri-
dors of the courts, Harald standing
back for his wife Claudia with the
politeness of a stranger as they found

the right court door, entered and shuffled clumsily sideways to be seated on the fixed benches.

The very smell of the place was that of a foreign country to which they were deported: the odour of polished wooden barriers and highly waxed floor. The windows high above, sloping down their search-lights. The uniforms occupied by men with the impersonality of cult members, all interchangeable wear-ers of the garb. The presence of a few figures seated somewhere near, the kind who stare from park benches or lie face-down in public gardens. The mind flutters from what confronts it, as a bird that has flown into a confined space does from wall to wall, there must be an opening. Harald collided against awareness of school, too far back to be consciously remembered; institutional smell and hard wood under his buttocks. Even the name of a master was blundered into; nothing from the past could be more remote than this present. In a flick of attention he saw Claudia rouse from her immobility to disconnect the beeper that kept her in touch with her surgery. She felt the distraction and turned her head to read his oblique glance: nothing. She gave the stiff smile with which one greets somebody one isn't sure one knows.

He comes up from the well of a

stairway between two policemen. Duncan. Can it be? He has to be recognised in a persona that doesn't belong to him as they knew him, have always known him – and who could identify him better? He is wearing dark-green jeans and a black cotton sweater. The kind of clothes he customarily wears, but the neat collar of a white shirt is turned down outside the neck of the sweater; this is the detail, token submission to the conventions expected by a court, that makes the connection of reality between the one they knew, *him*, and this other, flanked by policemen.

A blast of heat came over Harald, confusion like anxiety or anger, but neither. Some reaction that never before had had occasion to be called up.

Duncan, yes. He looked at them, acknowledging himself. Claudia smiled at him with lifted head, for everyone to see. And he inclined his head to her. But he did not look at his parents directly again during the proceedings that followed, except as his controlled, almost musing glance swept over them as it went round the public gallery across the two young black men with their legs sprawled relaxedly before them, the old white man sitting forward with his head in his hands, and the family group, probably wandered in bewilderedly to pass the time before a case that concerned them came up, who were whispering among themselves of their own affairs.

The judge made his stage entrance, everyone fidgeted to their feet, sank again. The judge was tall or short, bald or not – doesn't matter; there was the hitch of shoulders under the voluminous gown and, his hunch lowered over papers presented to him, he made a few brief comments in the tone of questions addressed to the tables in the well of the court where the backs of the prosecutor and defence lawyer presented themselves to the gallery. Under ladders of light tilting down, policemen on errands came in and out, conferring in hoarse whispers; the rote of proceedings was concluded. The case was remanded to a date two weeks later. A second application for bail was refused.

Over. But beginning. The parents approached the barrier between the gallery and the court enclosure and were not prevented from contact with their son. Each embraced him while he kept his head turned away from their faces.

Do you need anything?

It's just not on, the young lawyer was saying. I'm serving notice to contest the refusal, right away, right now, Duncan. I won't let the prosecutor get away with it. Don't worry. – This last said to her, the doctor, in exactly the tone of reassurance she herself would use with patients of whose prognosis she herself was uncertain.

The son had an air of impatience, the shifting gaze of one who wished the well-meaning to leave; an urgent need of some preoccupation, business with himself. They could take it to mean confidence; of his innocence – of course; or it could be a cover for dread, akin to the dread they had felt, concealing his dread out of pride, not wanting to be associated with theirs. He was now officially an accused, on record as such. The accused has a status of dread that is his own, hasn't he!

Nothing?

I'll see to everything Duncan needs – the lawyer squeezed his client's arm as he swung a briefcase and was off.

If there was nothing, then . . .

Nothing. Nothing they could ask, not *What is it all about*, what is it that you did; you are supposed to have done?

His father held and expelled a breath again as he had when he switched off the TV set. Is he really a competent enough lawyer? We could get someone else. Anyone.

A good friend and a good lawyer.

Well, I'll be in touch with him later, find out what happened when he saw the prosecutor.

The son will know that his father means money: he'll be ready to supply surety for the contingency that it is impossible to believe has arisen between them, money for bail.

He turns away – the prisoner, that's what he is now – in anticipation of the policemen's move to order him to. He doesn't want them to touch him, he has his own volition, and his mother's clasp just catches the ends of his fingers as he goes.

They see him led down the stairwell to whatever is there beneath the court. As they make to leave Court B17 they become aware that the other friend, the messenger

Julian, has been standing just behind
them, to assure Duncan of his presence but not wanting to intrude
upon those with the closest claims.
They greet him and walk out together but do not speak. He feels
guilty about his mission, that night,
and hurries ahead out of their sight.

As the couple emerge into the
foyer of the courts, vast and lofty
cathedral echoing with the susurra-
tion of its different kind of sup-
plicants gathered there, Claudia
suddenly breaks away, disappearing
towards the sign indicating toilets.
Harald waits for her among these
people patient in trouble, no choice
to be otherwise, for them; he is
one of them, the wives, husbands,

fathers, lovers, children of forgers, thieves and murderers. He looks at his watch. The whole process has taken exactly one hour and seven minutes. She returns and they quit the place,

Let's have a coffee somewhere.

Oh . . . There are patients at the surgery, expecting me.

Let them wait.

She did not have time to get to the lavatory and vomited in the wash-room basin. There was no warning; trooping out with all those other people in trouble, part of the anxious and stunned gait, she suddenly felt the clenching of her insides and knew what was going to come. She did not tell him, when she rejoined him, and he must have assumed she had gone to the place for the usual purpose. Medically, there was an explanation for such an attack coming on without nausea. Extreme tension could trigger the seizure of muscles. 'Vomited her heart out': that was the expression some of her patients used when describing the symptom. She had always received it, drily, as dramatically inaccurate.

Let them wait.

What he was saying was to hell with them, the patients, how can their pains and aches and pregnancies compare with this? Everything came to a stop, that night; everything has come to a stop. In the coffee bar an androgynous waiter with long curly hair tied back and tennis-ball biceps hummed his pleasure along with piped music. In the mortuary there was lying the body of a man. They ordered a filter coffee (Harald) and a *cappuccino* (Claudia). The man who was shot in the head, found dead. Why should it be unexpected that it was a man? Was not that a kind of admission, already, credence that it could have been done at all? To assume that the body would represent a woman, a woman killed out of jealous passion, the most common form of the act, one from the sensational pages of the Sunday

24

papers, *crime passionnel*, was to accept the possibility that it was committed, *entered at all* into a life's context. *His.* Road accidents, plane crashes, the random violence of night streets, these are the hazards that belong there, the contemporary version of what people used to believe in as fate, along with the given eternals, the risks of illness, failure of ambition, loss of love. These are what those responsible for an existence recognise they have exposed it to.

We're not much the wiser.

She didn't answer. Her eyebrows lifted as she reached for the packets of sugar. Her hand was trembling slightly, privately, from the recent violent convulsion of her body. If he noticed he did not remark on it.

They now understood what they had expected from *him*: outrage at the preposterous – thing – accusation, laid upon him. Against his presence there between two policemen before a judge. They had expected to have him burst forth at the sight of them; that was what they were ready for, to tell them – what? Whatever he could, within the restriction of that room with policemen hovering and clerks scratching papers together and the gallery hangers-on dawdling past. That his being there was crazy, they must get him out immediately, importune officials, protest –

what? Tell them. Tell them. Some explanation. How it could be thought that this situation was possible.

A good friend.

The lawyer a good friend. And that was all. His back as he went down the stairwell, a policeman on either side. Now, while Harald stretched a leg so that he could reach coins in his trouser pocket, *he* was in a confine they had never seen, a cell. The body of a man was in the mortuary. Harald left a tip for the young waiter who was humming. The petty rituals of living are a daze of continuity over what has come to a stop.

They were walking to their car

through the continuum of the city, separated and brought side by side again by the narrowing and widening of the pavements in relation to other people going about their lives, the vendors' spread stocks of small pyramids of vegetables, chewing gum, sunglasses and second-hand clothes, the gas burners on which sausages like curls of human gut were frying.

In the afternoon she couldn't let them wait. It was the day come round for her weekly stint at a clinic. Doctors like herself, in private practice, were expected to meet this need in areas of the city and the once genteel white suburbs of Johannesburg where now there was an influx, a rise in and variety of the population. Now conscientiousness goaded her, over what had come to a stop; she went to her clinic instead of accompanying Harald to the lawyer. Perhaps this also was to keep herself to the conviction that what had happened could not be? It was not a day to examine motives; just follow the sequence set out in an appointment register. She put on her same white coat (she's a functionary, as the judge is, hunched in his robe) and entered the institutional domain familiar to her, the steaming steriliser with its battery of precise instruments for every task, the dancing show of efficiency of the young district nurse with her doll's starched white crown pinned at the top of her dreadlocks.

The procession of flesh was laid before the doctor. It was her medium, in which she worked, the abundant black thighs reluctantly parted in modesty (the nurse chaffed the women, *Ma-gogo*, Doctor's a woman just like you), the white hairy paps of old men under auscultation. The babies' tender bellies slid under her palms; tears of terrible reproach bulged from their eyes when she had to thrust the needle into the soft padding of their upper arms, where muscle had not yet developed. She did it as she performed any necessary procedure, with all her skill to avoid pain.

Isn't that the purpose?

There is plenty of pain that arises from within; this woman with a tumour growing in her neck, plain to feel it under experienced fingers, and then the usual weekly procession of pensioners hobbled by arthritis.

But the pain inflicted from without – the violation of the flesh, a child is burned by an overturned pot of boiling water, or a knife is thrust. A bullet. This piercing of the flesh, the force, ram of a bullet deep into it, steel alloy that breaks bone as if shattering a teacup – she is not a surgeon but in this violent city she has watched those nuggets delved for and prised out on operating tables; they retain the streamline shape of velocity itself, there is no element in the human body that can withstand, even dent, a bullet – those who survive recall the pain differently from one another but all accounts agree: an assault. The pain that is the product of the body itself, its malfunction, is part of the self; somewhere, a mystery medical science cannot explain, the self is responsible. But this – the bullet in the head: the pure assault of pain.

The purpose of a doctor's life is to defend the body against the violence of pain. She stands on the other side of the divide from those who wilfully cause it. The divide of the ultimate, between death and life.

This body whose interior she is exploring with a plastic-gloved hand like a diviner's instinctively led to a hidden water-source has a foetus, three months of life inside it.

I'm telling you true, Doctor. I was never so sick with the others. Every morning, sick like a dog.

Vomit your heart out.

D'you think that means it's a boy, Doctor? The patient has the mock coyness women often affect towards a doctor; the consulting room is their stage for a little performance. Ag, my husband'd be over the moon for a boy. But I tell him, if we don't do it right this time, I don't know about you, but I'm giving up.

The doctor obliges by laughing with her.

We could do a simple test if you want to know the sex.

Oh no, it's God's will.

Life staggers along powered by worn bellows of old people's lungs and softly pulses between the ribs of a skinny small boy. For some, what is prescribed is denied them by circumstances outside their control. Green vegetables and fresh fruit – they are too poor for the luxury of these remedies; what they have come to the doctor for is a magical bottle of medicine. She knows this but has ready a supply of diet sheets which propose meals made with

various pulses as some sort of sub-
stitute for what they should be able
to eat. She hands a sheet encoura-
gingly to the woman who has
brought her two grandchildren to
the doctor. Their scarred grey-
filmed black legs are bare, but
despite the heat they watch the
doctor from under thick woollen
caps that cover the sores on their
heads and come down right to the
eyebrows. The woman studies the
sheet slowly at arm's length in the
manner of ageing people becoming
far-sighted. She folds it carefully.
Her time is up. She shepherds the
children to the door. She thanks the
doctor. I don't know if I can get.
Maybe I can try buy some these

things. The father, he's still in jail. My son.

Charge sheet. Indictment. Harald kept himself at a remove of cold attention in order to separate what was evidence from interpretation of that evidence. Circumstantial evidence: that day, that night, Friday 19th January, 1996, a man was found dead in a house he shared with two other men. David Baker and Nkululeko 'Kulu' Dladla came home at 6.45 p.m. and found the body of their friend Carl Jespers in the living room. He had a bullet wound in the head. He was lying half-on, half-off a sofa, as if (Interpretation) he had been taken by

surprise when shot and had tried to
rise. He was wearing thonged san-
dals, one of which was twisted
hanging off his foot, and above a
pair of shorts was naked. There were
two glasses on an African drum that
served as a table beside the sofa. One
held the dregs of what appeared to
have been a mixture known as a
Bloody Mary – an empty tin of
tomato juice and a bottle of vodka
were on top of the television set.
The other glass was apparently un-
used; there was an opened bottle of
whisky and a bucket of half-melted
ice on a tray on the floor beside the
drum. (Circumstantial combined
with Interpretation.) There was no
unusual disorder in the room; this is

a bachelor household. (Interpretation.) The room was in darkness except for the pinpoint of light from the CD player that had come to the end of a disc and not been disconnected. The front door was locked but glass doors which led to the garden were open. (Circumstantial.)

The garden is one in which a cottage is sited. The house is the main dwelling on a property common to both. The cottage is occupied by Duncan Linmeyer, a mutual friend of the dead man and the two men who discovered him, and they ran to Linmeyer after they had seen Jespers' body. Linmeyer's dog was asleep outside the cottage and it appeared that there was no one at home. When the police came about twenty minutes later they searched the garden and found a gun in a clump of fern. Baker and Dladla identified it as the gun kept in the house as mutual protection against burglars; neither could recall in whose of their three names it was licensed, if at all. A plumber's assistant, Petrus Muchanga, who occupied an outhouse on the property in exchange for part-time work in the garden, was questioned and said that he had seen Linmeyer come out on the verandah of the house and drop something as he crossed the garden to the cottage. Muchanga thought he would retrieve it for him but

could not find anything. Linmeyer
had already entered his cottage.
Muchanga does not own a watch.
He could not say what time this was;
the sun was down. The police then
proceeded to the cottage. There was
no response to the bell or knocking
on the front door, but Muchanga
insisted that Linmeyer was inside.
The police effected entry by for-
cing the kitchen door and found
that Linmeyer was in the bedroom.
He seemed dazed. He said he had
been asleep. Asked whether he
knew his friend Carl Jespers had
been attacked, he went 'white in
the face' (Interpretation) and de-
manded, Is he dead?

Fingerprint tests were inconclusive because Muchanga had recently watered the clump of fern. The fingerprints on the gun were largely obliterated by mud.

This is not a detective story. Harald has to understand that the mode of events that genre represents is actuality, this is the sequence of circumstantial evidence and interpretation by which a charge of murder is arrived. It is a matter of patricide and matricide. On Friday 19th January, 1996. He/she.

ALSO AVAILABLE AS BLOOMSBURY QUIDS

Jimmy and the Desperate Woman, D. H. Lawrence
Einstein's Dreams, Alan Lightman
Bright Lights, Big City, Jay McInerney
Debatable Land, Candia McWilliam
Bliss and Other Stories, Katherine Mansfield
The Garden Party and Other Stories, Katherine Mansfield
So Far from God, Patrick Marnham
Lies of Silence, Brian Moore
The Lonely Passion of Judith Hearne, Brian Moore
The Pumpkin Eater, Penelope Mortimer
Lives of Girls and Women, Alice Munro
The Country Girls, Edna O'Brien
Coming Through Slaughter, Michael Ondaatje
The English Patient, Michael Ondaatje
In the Skin of a Lion, Michael Ondaatje
Running in the Family, Michael Ondaatje
Let Them Call it Jazz, Jean Rhys
Wide Sargasso Sea, Jean Rhys
Keepers of the House, Lisa St Aubin de Téran
The Quantity Theory of Insanity, Will Self
The Pigeon, Patrick Süskind
The Heather Blazing, Colm Tóibín
Cocktails at Doney's and Other Stories, William Trevor
The Choir, Joanna Trollope
Angel, All Innocence, Fay Weldon
Oranges are not the only fruit, Jeanette Winterson
The Passion, Jeanette Winterson
Sexing the Cherry, Jeanette Winterson
In Pharaoh's Army, Tobias Wolff
This Boy's Life, Tobias Wolff
Orlando, Virginia Woolf
A Room of One's Own, Virginia Woolf

Selected poetry of Matthew Arnold
Selected poetry of William Blake
Selected poetry of Rupert Brooke
Selected poetry of Elizabeth Barrett Browning
Selected poetry of Robert Browning
Selected poetry of Robert Burns
Selected poetry of Lord Byron
Selected poetry of John Clare
Selected poetry of Samuel Taylor Coleridge
Selected poetry of Emily Dickinson
Selected poetry of John Donne
Selected poetry of John Dryden
Selected poetry of Thomas Hardy
Selected poetry of Robert Herrick
Selected poetry of Gerard Manley Hopkins
Selected poetry of John Keats
Selected poetry of Rudyard Kipling
Selected poetry of D. H. Lawrence
Selected poetry of Andrew Marvell
Selected poetry of John Milton
Selected poetry of Wilfred Owen
Selected poetry of Alexander Pope
Selected poetry of Christina Rossetti
Selected poetry of Walter Scott
Selected poetry of William Shakespeare
Selected poetry of P. B. Shelley
Selected poetry of Alfred Lord Tennyson
Selected poetry of Edward Thomas
Selected poetry of Walt Whitman
Selected poetry of Oscar Wilde
Selected poetry of William Wordsworth
Selected poetry of W. B. Yeats